Who ever heard of a tiger in a pink hat?!

Nicola
Stott McCourt
&
Leah-Ellen
Heming

little bee

One day a tiger went shopping.

The tiger bought
a pink hat.

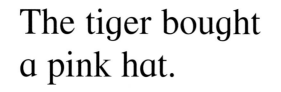

Fancy that, a pink hat!

Who ever heard of a tiger
in a pink hat?

Next the tiger bought
a stripy umbrella.

Well I never,
a stripy umbrella!

Who ever heard of a tiger with
a stripy umbrella?

Next the tiger bought some green gloves.

Heavens above,

green gloves!

Who ever heard of a tiger wearing **green gloves?**

Next the tiger bought
a banana split.

I don't believe it,
**a banana
split!**

Who ever heard of a tiger eating
a banana split?

Next the tiger bought
some French perfume.

You're joking I presume,

French
perfume?!

Who ever heard
of a tiger wearing
French perfume?

Next the tiger bought
some roller skates.

Let me get
this straight,
roller skates?!

Who ever heard of a tiger wearing
roller skates?

Next the tiger bought
a diamond ring.

How amazing,
a diamond ring!

Who ever heard of a tiger wearing
a diamond ring?

Next the tiger bought
a red sports car.

How bizarre,
a red sports car!
Who ever heard of a tiger driving
a red sports car?

Next the tiger
bought a fur coat.

Wow, take note,
    a fur coat!

Who ever heard
of a tiger in a
fur coat?!

Well, actually, I have!

For Mr McCourt
and my little men

N.M.

Pour mon ami Vincent

L.E.H.

First published in 2007 by Meadowside Children's Books

This edition published 2010 by Little Bee,
an imprint of Meadowside Children's Books, 185 Fleet Street, London EC4A 2HS
www.meadowsidebooks.com

A CIP catalogue record for this book
is available from the British Library
10 9 8 7 6 5 4 3 2

Printed in China